D0526490

This Bing book belongs to:

. . . .

90710 000 435 103

Copyright © 2020 Acamar Films Ltd

The *Bing* television series is created by Acamar Films and Brown Bag Films
and adapted from the original books by Ted Dewan

Original story written by Matthew Leys, Mikael Shields and Claire Jennings

Bing's Big Surprise was adapted from the original television script by Rebecca Gerlings

First published in the UK in 2020 by HarperCollins *Children's Books*
A division of HarperCollins Publishers Ltd, 1 London Bridge Street, London SE1 9GF

1 3 5 7 9 10 8 6 4 2

ISBN: 978-0-00-838162-2

Printed in China

MIX
Paper from
responsible sources
FSC www.fsc.org **FSC® C007454**

FSC ™ is a non-profit international organisation established to promote
the responsible management of the world's forests. Products carrying the
FSC label are independently certified to assure consumers that they come
from forests that are managed to meet the social, economic and
ecological needs of present and future generations,
and other controlled sources.

Find out more about HarperCollins and the environment at
www.harpercollins.co.uk/green

Bing's
Big Surprise

HarperCollins *Children's Books*

Round the corner, not far away,
Bing is making a playhouse today.

Bing and Sula pile
up the boxes, pots
and bottles on the
grass outside.

Bing looks back at the shed. "Is my playhouse ready yet?" he asks.

"*Our* playhouse," Pando and Sula giggle.

"Soon, Bing," promises Flop.
There's still lots to do.

Sula looks around. "What do we do with
all these things, Flop?" she asks.

"Well," replies Flop, "some we'll give away, some we'll have to throw out and some we can

recycle."

Pando doesn't know what recycling is, so Sula explains: "It's when you use something again, and don't throw it away."

Once the shed is empty, they rush to look inside.
"It's not very playhouse-y, is it, Bing?"
says Sula, feeling disappointed.

"Let's put this in!" suggests Bing,
spotting an old picnic blanket.

Sula and Pando find cushions and toys to bring in as well.

Now it feels more like a playhouse,
but something is still missing – lights!

Flop switches them on . . .

Click!

"Oh! Beautiful!" they all gasp.

"It needs **one other thing . . .**" says Bing,
looking around for **a quiet spot** for Hoppity's bed.

Sula helps Bing find the **perfect place** up on a shelf
in the corner. But **something else** is sitting on the shelf . . .

Wow!

"It's a birdie nest! With eggs!
Birdie eggs, Flop!"

Bing can't believe
his eyes. What
a surprise!

Pando and Sula can't wait to look at the eggs too.

"I want to see!" Sula exclaims.

"Can I see?" Pando asks,
excitedly jumping up and down.

Pando jumps
on to the crate.

"OK,"

says Flop
firmly. "Let's take
turns. Be gentle –
and careful –
not to touch the
nest, or the eggs.
Very Important."

It's Sula's turn now. "Oh, they're so pretty!
But where has the birdie gone?"

"Birdie!" calls Pando, laughing. "Birdie! *Biiiirdie!*"

"Shhh, Pando!" says Bing. "We've **scared** the birdie away!"

"Shhh!"

Sula has an idea. "Let's look outside!"

Bing, Sula, Pando and
Flop are super quiet as
they peep over the boxes
and up at the big tree . . .

"Ahhh, look!" says Bing.
"There she is! She's just a tiny birdie!"

"Shhh! Bing!" Sula reminds him.

TWEET! TWEET! TWEET!

The bird flies into the playhouse
through a little gap under the roof.

Bing rushes
into the playhouse,
but she isn't there!

"If we go in,
the birdie
won't go in!"
he realises.

"But . . ." adds Sula, "if the birdie doesn't stay with her eggs, they won't hatch into babies."

"Oh no!" says Bing. "No baby birdies!"

Bing, Pando and Sula feel very sad
at the idea of no baby birdies.

Suddenly, the little birdie sings again!

"Hello, Birdie!" everyone says, waving,
and listening to her pretty song.

TWEET!

TWEET!

TWEET!

"Maybe she's waiting to see what you will do?" suggests Flop.

Bing is quiet for a moment. "I think," he says, "we should let it be **her house**, Flop."

"That's **very kind** of you, Bing," says Flop.

"And then, when her babies have grown," Bing adds, "it can be **our playhouse again!**"

Bing closes the playhouse door and the little bird flies straight inside to her nest, tweeting her song.

TWEET!

TWEET!

TWEET!

"Oh, she's saying thank you, Bing!" says Sula, giggling.

"That's OK, Birdie," says Bing, smiling.

"But now we don't have a playhouse," says Pando.

Bing suddenly has an idea . . .

"The tent!" he cries. "We can use the tent!"

"Great idea!" says Flop, opening the tent with a

POP!

"YAY!" everyone cheers.

Pop!

Sharing your playhouse . . .
it's a Bing thing.